Music for
SHABBAT
WORSHIP

from the 69th URJ Biennial
December 14 - 15, 2007
San Diego, California

Editors:
Michael Boxer
Cantor Alane S. Katzew

Typesetter:
Josh Wiczer

Transcontinental Music Publications
The world's leading publisher of Jewish music since 1938

UNION FOR
REFORM JUDAISM
SERVING REFORM CONGREGATIONS IN NORTH AMERICA

URJ
FOR A LIFETIME OF

Please visit www.TranscontinentalMusic.com

Hebrew Pronunciation Guide

VOWELS

a as in f*a*ther
ai as in *ai*sle (= long *i* as in *i*ce)
e = short *e* as in b*e*d
ei as in *ei*ght (= long *a* as in *a*ce)
i as in p*i*zza (= long *e* as in b*e*)
o = long *o* as in g*o*
u = long *u* as in l*u*nar
' = unstressed vowel close to ə or unstressed short *e*
oi as in b*oy*

CONSONANTS

ch as in German Ba*ch* or Scottish lo*ch* (not as in *ch*eese)
g = hard *g* as in **g**et (not soft *g* as in **g**em)
tz = as in boa*ts*
h after a vowel is silent

Music for Shabbat Worship from the 69th URJ Biennial
Copyright © 2007 Transcontinental Music Publications
A Division of the Union for Reform Judaism
633 Third Avenue, New York, NY 10017- Fax 212.650.4119
212.650.4101 www.TranscontinentalMusic.com tmp@urj.org
993334

ISBN 0-8074-1084-5
10 9 8 7 6 5 4 3 2 1
Limited Edition
Printed in the United States

CONTENTS

Kabbalat Shabbat

Shabbat Shacharit

Music for
SHABBAT
WORSHIP

from the 69th URJ Biennial
December 14 - 15, 2007
San Diego, California

KABBALAT
SHABBAT

Mizmor L'David

Music: Shlomo Carlebach
Text: Psalm 29

מזמור לדוד

CD track ①

מִזְמוֹר לְדָוִד הָבוּ לַיהוָה בְּנֵי אֵלִים הָבוּ לַיהוָה כָּבוֹד וָעֹז.
הָבוּ לַיהוָה כְּבוֹד שְׁמוֹ הִשְׁתַּחֲווּ לַיהוָה בְּהַדְרַת־קֹדֶשׁ.
קוֹל יְהוָה עַל־הַמָּיִם אֵל־הַכָּבוֹד הִרְעִים.

A Psalm of David.
Ascribe to Adonai, O divine beings, ascribe to Adonai glory and strength. Ascribe to Adonai the glory of God's name; bow down to Adonai, majestic in holiness.

3

L'cha Dodi Medley

Music: Ashkenazic Folk Tune, Breslov Chassidic, A. Rotenberg
Text: Shlomo Alkabetz

לכה דודי

CD track ②

4

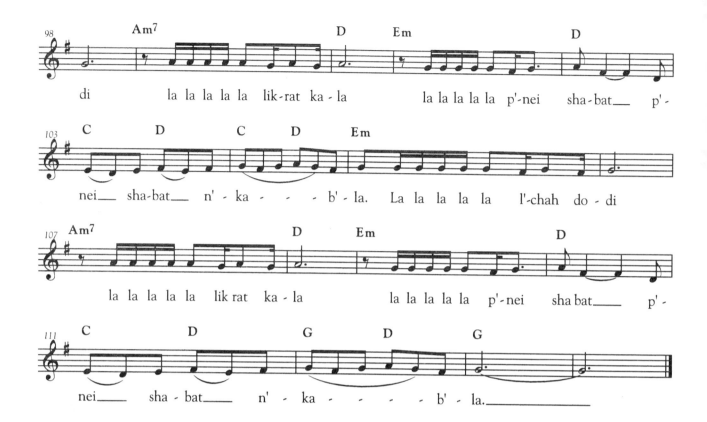

la la la la la lik-rat ka-la   la la la la la p'-nei sha-bat__ p'-

nei_ sha-bat__ n'-ka___b'-la. La la la la la l'-chah do-di

la la la la la lik rat ka-la   la la la la la p'-nei sha bat__ p'-

nei___ sha-bat___ n'-ka____b'-la.___

לְכָה דוֹדִי לִקְרַאת כַּלָּה פְּנֵי שַׁבָּת נְקַבְּלָה.

"שָׁמוֹר" וְ"זָכוֹר" בְּדִבּוּר אֶחָד
הִשְׁמִיעָנוּ אֵל הַמְּיֻחָד.
יְיָ אֶחָד וּשְׁמוֹ אֶחָד
לְשֵׁם וּלְתִפְאֶרֶת וְלִתְהִלָּה.

לִקְרַאת שַׁבָּת לְכוּ וְנֵלְכָה
כִּי הִיא מְקוֹר הַבְּרָכָה.
מֵרֹאשׁ מִקֶּדֶם נְסוּכָה
סוֹף מַעֲשֶׂה בְּמַחֲשָׁבָה תְּחִלָּה.

הִתְעוֹרְרִי, הִתְעוֹרְרִי,
כִּי בָא אוֹרֵךְ! קוּמִי אוֹרִי,
עוּרִי עוּרִי שִׁיר דַּבֵּרִי,
כְּבוֹד יְיָ עָלַיִךְ נִגְלָה.

בּוֹאִי בְשָׁלוֹם עֲטֶרֶת בַּעְלָהּ
גַּם בְּשִׂמְחָה וּבְצָהֳלָה.
תּוֹךְ אֱמוּנֵי עַם סְגֻלָּה.
בּוֹאִי כַלָּה! בּוֹאִי כַלָּה!

Come, my beloved, to greet the bride; let us welcome the Sabbath presence.

"Keep and "remember": a single command the Only God caused us to hear; the Eternal is One, God's Name is One; glory and praise are God's.

Come with me to meet Shabbat, forever a fountain of blessing. Still it flows, as from the start: the last of days, for which the first was made.

Awake, awake, your light has come! Arise, shine, awake and sing: the Eternal's glory dawns upon you.

Enter in peace, O crown of your husband, enter in gladness, enter in joy. Come to the people that keeps its faith. Enter, O bride! Enter, O bride!

Mizmor Shir L'Yom HaShabbat

מזמור שיר

Music: *Debbie Friedman*
Text: *Psalm 92*

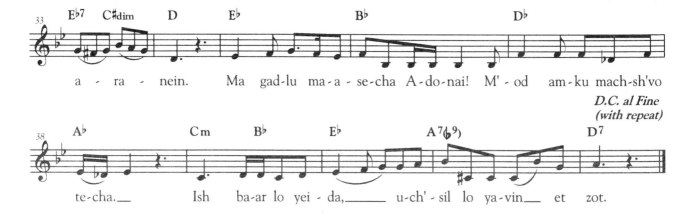

a - ra - nein. Ma gad-lu ma-a-se-cha A-do-nai! M'-od am-ku mach-sh'vo

D.C. al Fine
(with repeat)

te-cha.___ Ish ba-ar lo yei-da,_____ u-ch'-sil lo ya-vin__ et zot.

מִזְמוֹר שִׁיר לְיוֹם הַשַּׁבָּת. טוֹב לְהֹדוֹת לַיהוָה וּלְזַמֵּר לְשִׁמְךָ עֶלְיוֹן.
לְהַגִּיד בַּבֹּקֶר חַסְדֶּךָ וֶאֱמוּנָתְךָ בַּלֵּילוֹת. עֲלֵי-עָשׂוֹר וַעֲלֵי-נָבֶל עֲלֵי הִגָּיוֹן בְּכִנּוֹר.
כִּי שִׂמַּחְתַּנִי יְהוָה בְּפָעֳלֶךָ בְּמַעֲשֵׂי יָדֶיךָ אֲרַנֵּן. מַה-גָּדְלוּ מַעֲשֶׂיךָ יְהוָה מְאֹד
עָמְקוּ מַחְשְׁבֹתֶיךָ. אִישׁ-בַּעַר לֹא יֵדָע וּכְסִיל לֹא-יָבִין אֶת-זֹאת.

A psalm, a Song for Shabbat.

It is good to praise Adonai, to sing hymns
to Your name, O Most High, to proclaim
Your steadfast love at daybreak, Your
faithfulness each night, with a ten-stringed
harp, with voice and lyre together.

You have gladdened me by Your deeds,
Adonai; I shout for joy at Your
handiwork. How great are Your works,
Adonai, how very subtle Your designs!

A brute cannot know, a fool cannot
understand this.

Bar'chu

Music: *Rick Recht*
Text: *Liturgy*

בָּרְכוּ אֶת־יְיָ הַמְבֹרָךְ!
בָּרוּךְ יְיָ הַמְבֹרָךְ לְעוֹלָם וָעֶד!

Praise Adonai to whom praise is due forever!
Praised be Adonai to whom praise is due,
now and forever!

Copyright © Rick Recht

9

Maariv Aravim

Music: Stephen Richards
Text: Evening Liturgy

מעריב ערבים

CD track ⑤

בָּרוּךְ אַתָּה, יְיָ אֱלֹהֵינוּ, מֶלֶךְ הָעוֹלָם,
אֲשֶׁר בִּדְבָרוֹ מַעֲרִיב עֲרָבִים.
בְּחָכְמָה פּוֹתֵחַ שְׁעָרִים, וּבִתְבוּנָה מְשַׁנֶּה
עִתִּים וּמַחֲלִיף אֶת־הַזְּמַנִּים, וּמְסַדֵּר
אֶת־הַכּוֹכָבִים בְּמִשְׁמְרוֹתֵיהֶם בָּרָקִיעַ כִּרְצוֹנוֹ.
בּוֹרֵא יוֹם וָלַיְלָה, גּוֹלֵל אוֹר מִפְּנֵי חֹשֶׁךְ
וְחֹשֶׁךְ מִפְּנֵי אוֹר, וּמַעֲבִיר יוֹם וּמֵבִיא לַיְלָה,
וּמַבְדִּיל בֵּין יוֹם וּבֵין לַיְלָה יְיָ צְבָאוֹת שְׁמוֹ.
אֵל חַי וְקַיָּם, תָּמִיד יִמְלֹךְ עָלֵינוּ לְעוֹלָם וָעֶד.
בָּרוּךְ אַתָּה, יְיָ, הַמַּעֲרִיב עֲרָבִים.

Blessed are You, Adonai our God, Ruler of the universe, who speaks the evening into being, skillfully opens the gates, thoughtfully alters the time and changes the seasons, and arranges the stars in their heavenly courses according to plan. You are Creator of day and night, rolling light away from darkness and darkness from light, transforming day into night and distinguishing one from the other. Adonai Tz'vaot is Your Name. Ever-living God, may You reign continually over us into eternity. Blessed are You, Adonai, who brings on evening.

Sh'ma

Music: *Debbie Friedman*
Text: *Evening Liturgy, Deuteronomy 6:4*

שמע

CD track ⑥

Tenderly (♩ = 92)

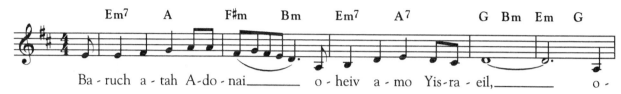

Ba - ruch a - tah A - do - nai_____ o - heiv a - mo Yis - ra - eil,_____ o -

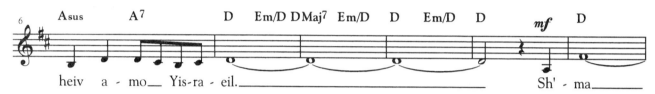

heiv a - mo_ Yis - ra - eil._____ Sh' - ma_____

_ Yis - ra - eil_____ A - do - nai_____ E - lo - hei - nu_ A - do -

nai_____ A - do - nai E - chad._____ Ba - ruch_____ sheim k' - vod_____

_ sheim k' - vod_____ mal' - chu - to_____ l' - o - lam_____

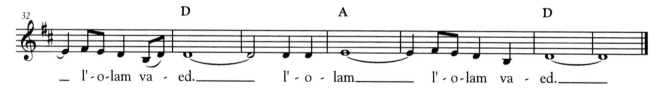

_ l' - o - lam va - ed._____ l' - o - lam_____ l' - o - lam va - ed._____

בָּרוּךְ אַתָּה, יְיָ, אוֹהֵב עַמּוֹ יִשְׂרָאֵל.

שְׁמַע יִשְׂרָאֵל: יְיָ אֱלֹהֵינוּ, יְיָ אֶחָד!
בָּרוּךְ שֵׁם כְּבוֹד מַלְכוּתוֹ לְעוֹלָם וָעֶד!

Praise to You, Adonai, who loves Your people Israel.

Hear, O Israel: Adonai is our God, Adonai is One!
Blessed is God's glorious majesty for ever and ever!

Mi-Chamocha / Miriam's Song

מי–כמכה

Music: *Debbie Friedman*
Text: *Mi-Chamocha: Exodus 15: 11, 18*
Miriam's Song: Debbie Friedman, Based on Exodus 15: 20-21

CD track ⑦

D B   F#m7   A   B   F#m7

And the wom-en danc - ing with their tim - brels fol - lowed Mir - iam as__

A   F#7   B   F#m7   A   B

__ she sang her song. Sing a song to the One__ whom we've ex - alt - ed.

D.C. al Fine

B   F#m7   B F#m7 B F#m7 B F#m7 B

Mir - iam and the wom en danced and danced the whole night long.__

מִי־כָמֹכָה בָּאֵלִם, יְיָ?
מִי כָּמֹכָה, נֶאְדָּר בַּקֹּדֶשׁ,
נוֹרָא תְהִלֹּת, עֹשֵׂה פֶלֶא?

מַלְכוּתְךָ רָאוּ בָנֶיךָ, בּוֹקֵעַ יָם לִפְנֵי מֹשֶׁה וּמִרְיָם;
"זֶה אֵלִי!" עָנוּ וְאָמְרוּ:
"יְיָ יִמְלֹךְ לְעוֹלָם וָעֶד!"

Who is like You, O God, among the gods that are worshipped? Who is like You, majestic in holiness, awesome in splendor, working wonders?

Your children witnessed Your sovereignty, the sea splitting before Moses and Miriam. "This is our God!" they cried. "Adonai will reign forever and ever!"

Oseh Shalom

עושה שלום

Music: *Steve Dropkin*
Text: *Liturgy - Birkat Shalom*

עֹשֶׂה שָׁלוֹם בִּמְרוֹמָיו, הוּא יַעֲשֶׂה שָׁלוֹם
עָלֵינוּ וְעַל כָּל־יִשְׂרָאֵל, וְעַל כָּל יוֹשְׁבֵי תֵבֵל,
וְאִמְרוּ: אָמֵן.

May the One who makes peace in the high heavens make peace for us, for all Israel and all who inhabit the earth. Amen.

15

Sow in Tears, Reap in Joy

Music: Debbie Friedman
Text: Debbie Friedman, based on Psalm 126

CD track (9)

Passionately (♩ = 130)

Those who sow,__ who sow in tears__ will reap in joy,__ will__

reap in joy.__ Those who sow,__ who sow in tears__ will reap, will

reap__ in__ joy. It's the song of the dream er, from a

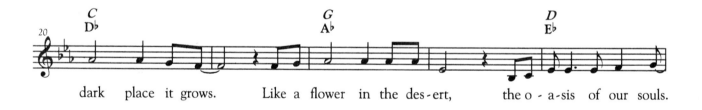

dark place it grows. Like a flower in the des-ert, the o-a-sis of our souls.

__ Come back,__ come back where we be-long,__ you who hear our

long-ing cries. Our mouths, our lips are filled with song. You can see our tear-filled eyes.

Am Yisraeil Chai

עם ישראל חי

Music: *Noam Katz*
Text: *unknown*

CD track ⑩

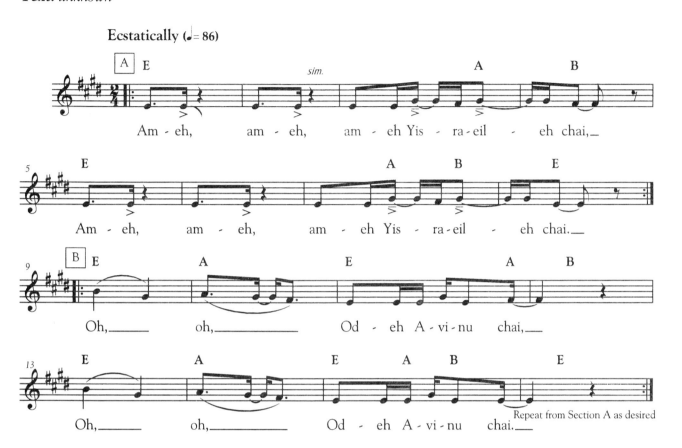

The people of Israel lives!
Our God yet lives!

17

SHABBAT SHACHARIT

Hinei Ma Tov / Nigun

הנה מה טוב

Music: *Abayudaya, Shlomo Carlebach*
Text: *Psalm 133:1*

CD track ⑪

הַנֵּה מַה־טּוֹב וּמַה־נָּעִים
שֶׁבֶת אַחִים גַּם־יָחַד.

How good and how pleasant it is that brothers and sisters dwell together.

Tzaddik Katamar

Music: *Louis Lewandowski*
Text: *Psalm 92: 13-16*

צדיק כתמר

CD track ⑫

צַדִּיק כַּתָּמָר יִפְרָח כְּאֶרֶז בַּלְּבָנוֹן יִשְׂגֶּה, שְׁתוּלִים בְּבֵית יְהֹוָה בְּחַצְרוֹת אֱלֹהֵינוּ יַפְרִיחוּ.
עוֹד יְנוּבוּן בְּשֵׂיבָה דְּשֵׁנִים וְרַעֲנַנִּים יִהְיוּ, לְהַגִּיד כִּי־יָשָׁר יְהֹוָה צוּרִי וְלֹא־עַוְלָתָה בּוֹ.

The righteous bloom like a date-palm; they thrive like a cedar in Lebanon;
planted in the house of Adonai, they flourish in the courts of our God.

In old age they still produce fruit; they are full of sap and freshness, attesting
that Adonai is upright, my Rock, in whom there is no wrong.

Psalm 150

Music: Debbie Friedman
Text: Psalm 150

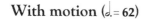

תהילים ק"נ

CD track ⑬

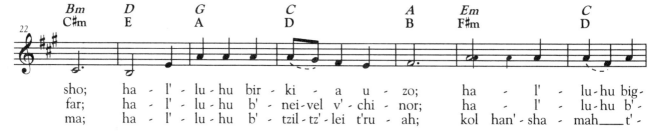

הַלְלוּ אֵל בְּקָדְשׁוֹ, הַלְלוּהוּ בִּרְקִיעַ עֻזּוֹ,
הַלְלוּהוּ בִגְבוּרֹתָיו, הַלְלוּהוּ כְּרֹב גֻּדְלוֹ.

הַלְלוּהוּ בְּתֵקַע שׁוֹפָר, הַלְלוּהוּ בְּנֵבֶל וְכִנּוֹר,
הַלְלוּהוּ בְּתֹף וּמָחוֹל, הַלְלוּהוּ בְּמִנִּים וְעֻגָב.

הַלְלוּהוּ בְצִלְצְלֵי שָׁמַע, הַלְלוּהוּ בְּצִלְצְלֵי תְרוּעָה.
כֹּל הַנְּשָׁמָה תְּהַלֵּל יָהּ, כֹּל הַנְּשָׁמָה תְּהַלֵּל יָהּ.

*Hallelu Yah! Praise God in the sanctuary; praise the
One whose power the heavens proclaim. Praise God for
mighty acts, praise the One for surpassing greatness.*

*Praise with shofar blast, praise with harp and lute, praise
with drum and dance, praise with strings and pipe.*

*Praise with cymbals sounding, praise with cymbals
resounding! Let all that breathes praise God!
Hallelu Yah!*

Let Us Honor the Generations

Music: Michael Isaacson
Text: Richard Levy

CD track ⑭

Mi-Chamochah

מִי־כָמְכָה

Music: Allan E. Naplan, adapted by Cantor Alane Katzew
Text: Exodus 15:11,18

Mi - cha - mo - chah__ ba-ei - lim A - do - nai?__ Mi__ ka - mo - chah__ ne-e-

dar__ ba-ko-desh, No-ra t'-hi-lot,__ o - seh fe - leh? Mi - cha-mo-chah ba-ei-

lim A - do - nai?_____ __ Shi - rah cha-da-shah____ shib

chu ge-u-lim l'-shim-cha___ al s'fat ha - yam__ ya-chad ku - lam ho-du

v'-him li - chu v'-am - ru: A do - nai__ yim - loch l'-o - lam, l'-o - lam_ va - ed.__

מִי־כָמְכָה בָּאֵלִם, יְיָ?
מִי כָּמְכָה, נֶאְדָּר בַּקֹּדֶשׁ,
נוֹרָא תְהִלֹת, עֹשֵׂה פֶלֶא?

שִׁירָה חֲדָשָׁה שִׁבְּחוּ גְאוּלִים
לְשִׁמְךָ עַל שְׂפַת הַיָּם
יַחַד כֻּלָּם הוֹדוּ וְהִמְלִיכוּ וְאָמְרוּ:

"יְיָ יִמְלֹךְ לְעוֹלָם וָעֶד!"

Who is like you, O God, among the gods that are worshipped? Who is like you, majestic in holiness, extolled in praises, working wonders?

With new song, inspired, at the shore of the sea, the redeemed sang Your praise. In unison they all offered thanks. Acknowledging Your Sovereignty, they said:

"Adonai will reign forever!"

S'fatai Tiftach

שפתי תפתח

Music: Hannah Tiferet Siegel

Text: Psalm 51:17

CD track ⑯

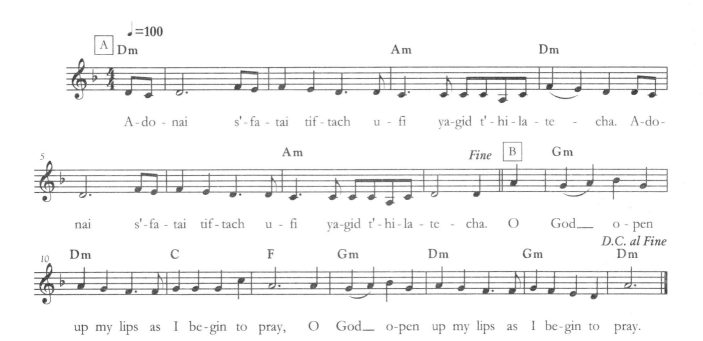

A-do-nai s'-fa-tai tif-tach u-fi ya-gid t'-hi-la-te-cha. A-do-nai s'-fa-tai tif-tach u-fi ya-gid t'-hi-la-te-cha. O God___ o-pen up my lips as I be-gin to pray, O God___ o-pen up my lips as I be-gin to pray.

אֲדֹנָי, שְׂפָתַי תִּפְתָּח וּפִי יַגִּיד תְּהִלָּתֶךָ.

Adonai, open up my lips, that my mouth may declare Your praise.

25

L'dor Vador

Music: Meir Finkelstein
Text: Morning Liturgy - Amidah

לְדוֹר וָדוֹר נַגִּיד גָּדְלֶךָ, וּלְנֵצַח נְצָחִים קְדֻשָּׁתְךָ נַקְדִּישׁ, וְשִׁבְחֲךָ, אֱלֹהֵינוּ,
מִפִּינוּ לֹא יָמוּשׁ לְעוֹלָם וָעֶד, כִּי אֵל מֶלֶךְ גָּדוֹל וְקָדוֹשׁ אָתָּה. בָּרוּךְ אַתָּה יְיָ, הָאֵל הַקָּדוֹשׁ.

*To all generations we will declare Your greatness, and for all
eternity proclaim Your holiness. Your praise, O God, shall
never depart from our lips.
Blessed are You, Adonai, the Holy God.*

Yihiyu L'ratzon

Music: *Ernest Bloch*
Text: *Psalm 19:15*

יהיו לרצון

CD track ⑱

יְהִיוּ לְרָצוֹן אִמְרֵי־פִי וְהֶגְיוֹן לִבִּי לְפָנֶיךָ, יְיָ, צוּרִי וְגוֹאֲלִי.

May the words of my mouth and the meditations of my heart be acceptable to You, Adonai, my Rock and my Redeemer.

Copyright © the composer

27

Oseh Shalom

עושה שלום

Music: Michael Hunter Ochs, arr. Eliot Glaser
Text: Liturgy - Birkat Shalom

CD track ⑲

28

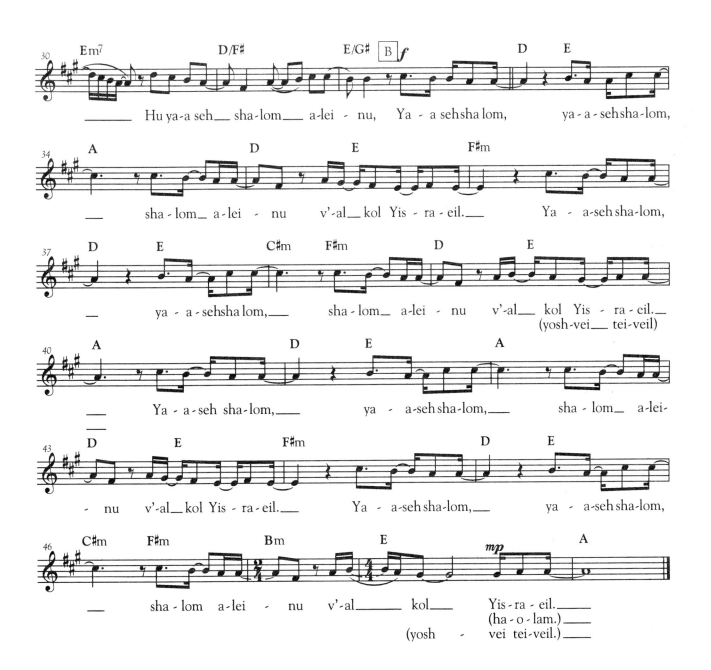

עֹשֶׂה שָׁלוֹם בִּמְרוֹמָיו, הוּא יַעֲשֶׂה שָׁלוֹם
עָלֵינוּ וְעַל כָּל־יִשְׂרָאֵל, וְעַל כָּל יוֹשְׁבֵי תֵבֵל,
וְאִמְרוּ: אָמֵן.

May the One who makes peace in the high heavens make peace for us, for all Israel and all who inhabit the earth. Amen.

S'u Sh'arim

Music: *Aminadav Aloni*
Text: *Psalm 24: 9-10*

שאו שערים

CD track ⃝20

שְׂאוּ שְׁעָרִים רָאשֵׁיכֶם וּשְׂאוּ פִּתְחֵי עוֹלָם וְיָבֹא מֶלֶךְ הַכָּבוֹד.
מִי הוּא זֶה מֶלֶךְ הַכָּבוֹד יְהֹוָה צְבָאוֹת הוּא מֶלֶךְ הַכָּבוֹד סֶלָה.

*Lift up your heads, O gates! Lift yourselves up, O
ancient doors! Let the Sovereign of glory enter. Who
is this Sovereign of glory? The God of Hosts is the
Sovereign of glory!*

Mi Shebeirach

Music: *Debbie Friedman, arr. Elliot Z. Levine*
Text: *Debbie Friedman and Drorah Setel*

מי שברך

CD track (21)

מִי שֶׁבֵּרַךְ אֲבוֹתֵינוּ מְקוֹר הַבְּרָכָה לְאִמּוֹתֵינוּ.
מִי שֶׁבֵּרַךְ אִמּוֹתֵינוּ מְקוֹר הַבְּרָכָה לַאֲבוֹתֵינוּ.

V'neemar/Bayom Hahu

ונאמר–ביום ההוא

Music: *Aminadav Aloni*
Text: *Zechariah 14:9*

CD track ㉒

Rubato (♩ = ca. 52)

V' - ne - e - mar v' - ha - yah A - do nai l' - me - lech al kol ha - a - retz. ___

Tempo (♩ = 126)

Ba - yom ha - hu ba - yom ha - hu ba - yom ha - hu ba -

yom ha - hu ba - yom ha - hu ba - yom ha - hu ba - yom ha - hu ba - yom ha - hu ba -

yom ha - hu yih' - yeh A - do - nai e - chad. Ba -

yeh A - do - nai e - chad u - sh' - mo e - chad.

וְנֶאֱמַר: וְהָיָה יְיָ לְמֶלֶךְ עַל־כָּל־הָאָרֶץ,
בַּיּוֹם הַהוּא יִהְיֶה יְיָ אֶחָד וּשְׁמוֹ אֶחָד.

Thus it has been said: "Adonai will be Sovereign over all the earth.
On that day, Adonai will be One and God's name will be One."

V'imru Amen

Music: *Bonia Shur*
Text: *Liturgy*

ואמרו: אָמֵן.   *To which we say: Amen.*

33

Ein Keiloheinu

אין כאלהינו

Music: Sephardic
Text: Liturgy

CD track (24)

Majestically (♩ = 128)

1. Ein k'Ei-lo-hei-nui, ein k'A-do-nei-nu, ein k'-Mal-kei-nu,
2. Mi ch'Ei-lo-hei-nu? Mi ch'A-do-nei-nu? Mi ch'-Mal-kei-nu?
3. No-dehl'Ei-lo-hei-nu, no-dehl'A-do-nei-nu, no-deh l'-Mal-kei-nu,
4. Ba ruch E-lo-hei-nu, ba ruch A-do-nei-nu, ba-ruch Mal-kei-nu,

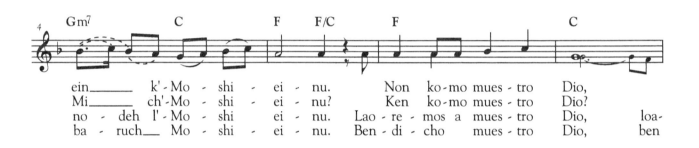

ein_____ k'-Mo-shi-ei-nu. Non ko-mo mues-tro Dio,
Mi_____ ch'-Mo-shi-ei-nu? Ken ko-mo mues-tro Dio?
no-deh l'-Mo-shi-ei-nu. Lao-re-mos a mues-tro Dio, loa
ba-ruch__ Mo-shi-ei-nu. Ben-di-cho mues-tro Dio, ben

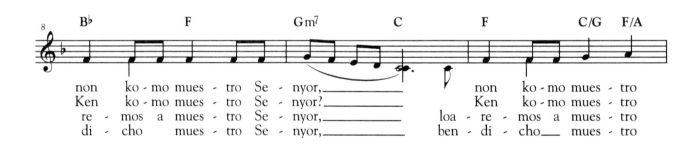

non ko-mo mues-tro Se-nyor,_____ non ko-mo mues-tro
Ken ko-mo mues-tro Se-nyor?_____ Ken ko-mo mues-tro
re-mos a mues-tro Se-nyor,_____ loa-re-mos a mues-tro
di-cho mues-tro Se-nyor,_____ ben-di-cho__ mues-tro

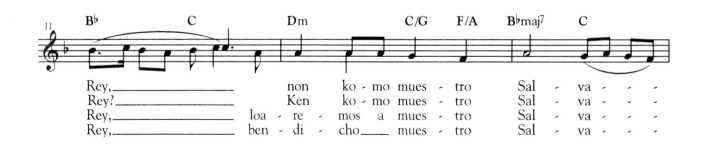

Rey,_____ non ko-mo mues-tro Sal-va - - -
Rey?_____ Ken ko-mo mues-tro Sal-va - - -
Rey,_____ loa-re-mos a mues-tro Sal-va - - -
Rey,_____ ben-di-cho__ mues-tro Sal-va - - -

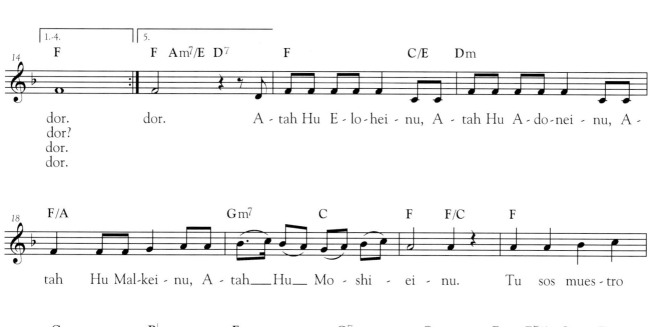

dor.
dor.
dor?
dor.
dor.

A - tah Hu E - lo - hei - nu, A - tah Hu A - do - nei - nu, A -

tah Hu Mal - kei - nu, A - tah__ Hu__ Mo - shi - ei - nu. Tu sos mues - tro

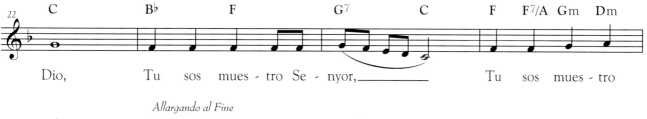

Dio, Tu sos mues - tro Se - nyor,_____ Tu sos mues - tro

Allargando al Fine

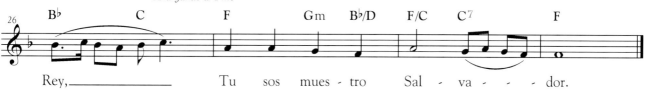

Rey,_____ Tu sos mues - tro Sal - va - - - dor.

אֵין כֵּאלֹהֵינוּ, אֵין כַּאדוֹנֵינוּ,	There is none like our God, there is none like our Eternal One;
אֵין כְּמַלְכֵּנוּ, אֵין כְּמוֹשִׁיעֵנוּ.	There is none like our Ruler, there is none like our Redeemer.
מִי־כֵאלֹהֵינוּ? מִי־כַאדוֹנֵינוּ?	Who is like our God? Who is like our Eternal One?
מִי־כְמַלְכֵּנוּ? מִי־כְמוֹשִׁיעֵנוּ?	Who is like our Ruler? Who is like our Redeemer?
נוֹדֶה לֵאלֹהֵינוּ, נוֹדֶה לַאדוֹנֵינוּ,	We will give thanks to our God, we ill give thanks to our Eternal One;
נוֹדֶה לְמַלְכֵּנוּ, נוֹדֶה לְמוֹשִׁיעֵנוּ.	We will give thanks to our Ruler, we will give thanks to our Redeemer.
בָּרוּךְ אֱלֹהֵינוּ, בָּרוּךְ אֲדוֹנֵינוּ,	Praised be our God, praised be our Eternal One;
בָּרוּךְ מַלְכֵּנוּ, בָּרוּךְ מוֹשִׁיעֵנוּ.	Praised be our Ruler, praised be our Redeemer.
אַתָּה הוּא אֱלֹהֵינוּ, אַתָּה הוּא אֲדוֹנֵינוּ,	You are our God, You are our Eternal One;
אַתָּה הוּא מַלְכֵּנוּ, אַתָּה הוּא מוֹשִׁיעֵנוּ.	You are our Ruler, You are our Redeemer.